How To Analyze People

Learn How To Analyze People: How To Read People Instantly Using Body Language, Psychological Techniques, & Personality

Christian Vaher

Table Of Contents

Introduction

Thank you for taking the time to download this book: *How To Analyze People: How To Read People Instantly Using Body Language, Psychological Techniques, & Personality*.

This book covers the topic of how to make quick and accurate deductions about people. It will teach you the science and phenomenon behind reading body language, how cold readings work, as well as nonverbal cues that can help you determine many things about an individual.

Have you ever been in a crowd of people and wondered what someone was thinking? Maybe you were on a date and had no idea what they thought of you? Or maybe your spouse is being cryptic about their daily habits and you wish you understood why? The truth is that people are mysteries, and lying can become just as much a habit as chewing gum or smoking. This means it can be hard to not merely understand a person, but to also know what their true intentions are.

If you ever found yourself wishing that you could read someone's mind, then look no further: while human beings are a complex organism, their emotions and body language are simple. There are nonverbal cues that give away emotional states, as well as involuntary cues that can give away what a person is truly thinking in the moment.

We live in a very social world, but technology has made it very difficult to discern between genuine communication and distractive communication. Whether we want to admit it or not, we are tied to every single person on the planet via our thoughts, our DNA, and the ways our bodies react to specific emotional states... and the real truth of the matter is that we cannot continue to live our lives and progress in this world without genuinely understanding one another.

No matter how much someone wants to put up a wall to the truth.

So, what is the benefit of being able to read someone? What good could come of something like that? For starters, it has many professional advantages: being able to read your coworkers, or even your boss, will help guide decisions you make on a day-to-day basis, in regard to your career. It also has social benefits, such as being able to read a room and learn how to control and command the room's attention. You can also use it as a tool to get closer to others, because what will come off as empathy will actually be your developed ability to read a person's own nonverbal and involuntary bodily cues. This can help you foster lifelong friendships, despite the fact that some might feel "cold reading" is an invasion of privacy.

At the completion of this valuable book, you will have a good understanding of why it is important to be able to analyze individuals, and be able to fully use the techniques outlined to begin bolstering your own interpersonal interactions. Whether it is your professional life or your personal life, you will soon be able to quickly recognize specific signals that will help you better communicate and evaluate situations around you.

If you have ever wondered what someone was thinking or feeling, or have ever felt socially uncomfortable, then this book is for you.

Once again, thank you so much for downloading this book, and I hope you find it to be motivating, helpful, and life-changing!

Chapter 1: Personality Types

While many people believe the Myers-Briggs personality test is full of unscientific mumbo-jumbo, it is important to understand that the 16 personality types it outlines are valid. The test was developed to assign specific people psychological types, based on C.G. Jung and his research, for people to better understand themselves.

The theory behind it is that behavior we view as chaotic or inconsistent is actually quite the opposite, and it all routes back to someone's personality type.

How someone perceives themselves is imperative to being able to perceive and interpret things about others. This is because it requires getting rid of personal biases about yourself, in order to truly self-analyze your psychological state and personality type.

Once you can assess yourself, it gets easier to peel away the layers of someone else, simply by analyzing them and their body language. This is because you have already started to learn the analysis techniques on yourself.

You are your own guinea pig, so to speak.

Perception then leads to judgement, and the 16 personality types help with judgement calls, when one is analyzing others. While judgement involves coming to specific conclusions, it is the perception someone has of another, that aids those judgement calls.

Becoming aware of people and their surroundings, can help you deduce what is really going on. It is critical to use both of these concepts, perception and judgement, in tandem with one another, in order to be accurate.

Otherwise, you are simply taking a weighted guess.

The Myers-Briggs personality test was developed specifically to identify an individual as one of the 16 outlined personality types, and then choose viable career and social paths for them, in terms of how they were categorized.

Everything from social and familial interaction, to successful career paths, were outlined once someone could dive into the intricacies of their personality.

The four major sections evaluated in this test give way to an either/or choice, depending on how the person taking the test answers the questions.

The first personality trait gauged is an individual's "favorite world." This simply means whether someone prefers the external world or the internal world, giving them a label of "extraversion" or "introversion."

The second one measured is "information." This means to gauge whether someone prefers focusing their time and energies on basic information or whether they choose to add their own specific meanings. This gives them a label of "sensing" or "intuition."

Third, decision-making is measured. Does someone prefer to look logically at a situation, or do they prefer to look at the people within the situation and take into account special, or extenuating, circumstances? This gives way to a label of "thinking" or "feeling."

Finally, the last trait measured is "structure," and this has to do with how people deal with the outside world. Does someone enjoy deciding things or do they prefer to stay open to options? This brings about a label of either "judging" or "perceiving."

The first thing to understand is that there is no "superior type." All 16 personality combinations are equal under this test, and it only means so show why a person acts the way they do, and why they would thrive in some environments and sink in others. It is not a measure of character or ability, it is simply a way to give insight into how someone thinks, interprets, and interacts with the world around them.

What does any of this have to do with analyzing people? Well, understanding how these eight subcategories interact with one another helps when it comes to observing how others interact in specific settings.

For example, someone who is more extroverted is more liable to part a crowd walking towards them, whereas someone who is more introverted might be seen weaving in and out of people. Understanding these basic definitions can help form the foundation of knowledge you will need, so you can begin to understand what it is you are observing.

Contrary to popular belief, personality types don't change over time. Once the brain has hardwired itself to react in a specific way and draw energy from specific resources, that part of a person is solidified. Unless a traumatic event occurs that brings about drastic worldview changes, a personality does not change.

So, what are the basic ideas of the eight subcategories? What do they mean?

The two most misinterpreted categories are defining an introvert versus defining an extravert. The misconception is that an extravert is loud and bombastic while an introvert is shy and reserved. This is not only inaccurate, it is not how you define introversion versus extraversion.

An introvert gathers their strength and energy by being alone, while an extravert gains their energy from others. It is possible for an introvert to go to a party, jump around and have a good time, engage in wonderful conversation, and then go home feeling fulfilled. But, they then need to retreat to a place where they are alone and have quiet, in order to refuel their energy stores.

Extraverts, on the other hand, gain their energy by engaging with these same people, and can sometimes even become restless when alone and in quiet places.

The next two subcategories are sensing versus intuition. When someone is a "sensor," they place more stock in what their bodily senses can input. They trust what they can see, hear, smell, taste, and touch, and solve problems by creating logical points from one end of the spectrum to another.

But, someone who is more intuitive pays more attention to patterns, individual impressions of others, and solves problems by thinking them through. Those people who are better at "reading between the lines" are seen as more intuitive, and can often see the bigger picture beyond the basic facts and outlines presented to them.

The decision-making section takes into account how someone takes their surroundings and comes to overall conclusions. Someone who is more of a "thinker" enjoys boiling a situation down to a specific truth or notion. They take the logical approach to their decision-making skills by using pro-and-con structures, and they are usually very good at not allowing someone's personal wishes, or even their own wishes, to influence their overall decision-making.

However, someone who is more of a "feeler" in their decision-making process takes the standpoint that decisions cannot be made without weighing these points-of-view and taking them into consideration. They are less concerned with the overall decision and more concerned with the values of the people involved with the decision.

Then, there is the last subset of categories, and it deals with the difference between "judging" and "perceiving." If someone is a "judger," they prefer an orderly and planned way of life. Routines are ingrained into them and they desperately need things to be settled and organized on a daily basis. Keep in mind, "judger" does not hold a negative connotation in this personality subset. It has nothing to do with someone being overly judgmental of others and their actions.

However, if someone is more of a "perceiver," they usually lead a more flexible and spontaneous life. Routines are not something they intentionally seek out, and they handle surprises better than those who fall underneath the "judging" subheading. Rather than trying to organize the world, they are better at adapting to it.

Committing these eight personality subcategories to memory will help you to begin categorizing what you see when you are analyzing someone. When you read someone and their body language, it is simply taking what you witness and putting a title to it.

 For example, if you see someone fidgeting with their hands while someone is talking at them, you might draw the conclusion that they are uncomfortable. If you see their shoulders caving in, trying to close themselves off to the person talking to them, you might view that as a signal of introversion. It might not mean they are inherently introverted, but it means, in that particular instance, they are wanting to be left alone rather than be surrounded by that individual.

Maybe you know someone in your family who needs constant structure, or who is obsessed with routines. Up until this point, maybe you recognized it, but didn't know what type of label to put on it.

Now you do.

Your first task is to go sit in a park, or on a bench in your local mall, and watch people. Commit these eight subcategories to mind and see how many accurate labels you can attach to someone merely by watching how they move and interact with their surroundings.

If it is hard at first, don't get upset with yourself. No one is asking you to figure out where they were yesterday by the dirt on their shoe, we are merely asking you to put certain labels to their actions in order to accurately draw an assumption of an underlying personality trait.

Chapter 2: How Personality Type Affects Communication

When it comes to analyzing people, part of the process is knowing how to communicate with them. When people think of analyzing others, they may think of the Sherlock Holmes type of characters that can deduce where someone was four hours ago based on the dust on their collar. But, part of analyzing people is learning how to determine what they really mean and feel when they verbally communicate.

And in order to do this, you have to be able to accurately communicate with everyone.

Have you ever wondered why in the world you can get along well with someone and be absolutely irritated by another? Maybe there's that person where the smallest utterance of a word sets your blood boiling, and you really aren't sure why!

If this happens to you, you're not being rash (unless they've wronged you in some way, of course). What's happening is that you are responding innately to their type of communicative ways in regard to how you communicate with them. It all boils down to two people's personality styles and how they interact with one another.

With communication, there are four basic personality types: conscientious, steady, influential, and dominant. Figuring out your communicative personality type will help you to figure out how it is that you communicate best, and it will also help you to discern how someone else communicates, so you can more accurately and effectively communicate with them.

After all, if you are wanting to analyze someone, but you can't do it verbally, you are missing 50% of the information you need to make your deductions in the first place!

The dominant communicator is someone who is considered vocal in their opinions, adventurous in their suggestions, and possibly even demanding or competitive. They are usually the ones designated to be project leaders and can often come across as rude or hurried.

The dominant communicator is often one that gets on many people's nerves. He or she will constantly interrupt people mid-sentence to interject what they feel or how they see things, and everyone around them knows their opinions.

Influential communicators are seen as the "social butterflies." They enjoy verbal communication with others and often joke around with those they are talking with. They come across as very open, excited, and warm with everyone they meet. This type of communicative personality is usually seen in someone who is unflinchingly positive in most situations.

Steady communicators are calculated and logical in the way they communicate. They enjoy their routines, absolutely hate distractions when talking, and do not like communicating until they have all the facts at hand to present their case.

Steady communicators tend to be quieter communicators, and are wonderful listeners when the communication is one-on-one. People who have this type of communicative personality are rarely ever jealous, and are good with keeping their emotions in-check during heated discussions.

Then, there are the conscientious communicators. They are precise and enjoy perfection, and are usually hard on themselves when they talk. They follow the rules to the furthest extent possible, and are usually not too expressive in person.

Conscientious communicators are the people that are better at communication via writing, than they are communication verbally. Because of this, they may come across as distant and cold, but that is not the case. These types of communicators don't enjoy being wrong or being disagreed with, so they usually just keep what they are thinking and feeling to themselves.

However, understanding what these four communicative personality types involve isn't enough, and neither is pinpointing how you communicate yourself. You also have to find a way to tailor your own communication style to the other three, in order to make someone feel comfortable enough around you to express themselves.

Remember, the entire point of knowing this information is not just to be able to pinpoint it, but to be able to get someone to open up to you so you can better analyze them, no matter how their communication style molds, or clashes, with yours.

A dominant communicator enjoys verbal recognition for their thoughts, conclusions, and actions. This means communicating with this type of person is going to take a lot of energy and verbal jousting.

Don't focus too much on problems or negative points with someone like this. They aren't interested in the small details, either. If you stick to the bigger picture, they will perceive you as a positive force and continue to communicate with you. Speak confidently with them and try to avoid rambling.

If you find yourself talking with an influential communicator, try not to talk as much as you would with a dominant one. If someone else wants to join in on the conversation, welcome it, because the influential communicator will. Keep your physical distance from them and give them their own space, and don't derail the conversation down a path it shouldn't take. Stick to the topic and allow them the space to express their side, and you will be in this communicator's good graces.

A steady communicator will require a counterpart that is more animated in their discussions without being too emotional. You can't be afraid to talk about things you might be unfamiliar with, because a steady communicator will expect you to keep up, but they won't always focus on the details. Keep your expression and animation separate from your emotions with this communicator, and you will be golden in their eyes.

A conscientious communicator needs a breadth of room to talk without being prodded for too many details. With this communicator, if they get going, let them run. Don't interject with questions of your own, and don't expect them to elaborate with facts or statistics to back up how they feel or perceive things around them.

Only add to the conversation when necessary, and always make sure you iterate that they are right in how they feel towards a situation, because they moment you tell them they aren't, they will shut down, and communication will cease.

Once you pinpoint the type of communicator you are, start your journey by prompting conversations with strangers. Sometimes they will brush you off, but sometimes they will reciprocate. If they do, see if you can nail down their communication personality type. In the beginning, it will simply be about labeling them.

Once you can accurately gauge how someone communicates, and use that information to tailor your own communication tactics with them, then you can move on to making basic deductions about them.

But, you will also be able to make basic deductions based on what people don't tell you. While verbally talking with someone is imperative in analyzing people, it is only 50% of what analyzing someone is.

The other 50% is comprised of body language, and involuntary actions.

Chapter 3: Does 'Criminal Minds' Get It Right?

There are many shows on television today that depict some form of expertise in interpreting body language. *Lie To Me* is a show about a man who considers himself a "human lie detector." *Criminal Minds* stems around an entire professional police force that analyzes people, and makes accurate predictions, based upon their psychological profiles.

So, what is the common thread between these two shows?

It's simple: body language.

When someone is attempting to read body language, the basic goal is to figure out whether a person is currently comfortable in the situation you've put them in. Then, it's a process of using other cues and contextual atmospheres in order to figure out specifics.

Within the basics of body language, there are two major categories: positive body language and negative body language. Positive body language consists of someone moving closer to you while you are talking, someone who is relaxed or is not crossing their arms, long periods of eye contact without a massive amount of blinking, and genuine smiles. While this is not inclusive of all of the positive body language someone can present, these are the basics that are easy to pinpoint.

Negative body language consists of someone moving away from you while you are talking to them, crossing their arms, bracing their body, pointing their extremities away from you (or towards an exit), or constantly rubbing their nose or the back of their neck. Like we said, these are not all of them, but they are the easiest to pinpoint for beginners.

Now, if you register one of these cues while you are interacting with someone, it can mean a variety of things. Sometimes a person can cross their arms because they are not interested in talking with you, or it could mean they have just had too much to eat. This is when the contextual atmosphere of the situation comes into play: if there is no food around and someone is crossing their arms, it's safe to say they probably have not eaten too much.

However, if the room is chilly, that might also be a reason they are crossing their arms.

Understanding someone's body language is not simply about the moves they make, it is also about the surroundings you find yourself in. This is why it's very important to make sure you understand the situation you have found yourself in. Someone will not communicate with you in a park the same way they might in a church.

Fusing the atmosphere as well as physical cues can then give way to the deeper meaning of someone's movements, or even words.

When someone wants to read another person, most of the time they are trying to figure out whether someone is lying to them or not. Do you think your spouse is cheating? Is your best friend standing you up a lot? Is your mom or dad doing things that seem odd or out-of-place? Whatever the scenario, paying attention to the physical bodily clues they give you when you are interacting with them will tell a lot about their psychological state of mind, as well as their true mood.

When trying to figure out if someone is lying, understand this: the same cues you get when someone is telling a lie because they are frightened, are not going to always be the same cues you get when someone is, say, lying by omission. Something as nuanced as lying by omission, or even exaggeration, takes a great deal of practice.

However, there are a few things you can easily pinpoint that will get you started honing your skills in order to become a master at deciphering other people via their body language.

Fake smiles are the first clue. The general rule of thumb is that a smile not only affects the cheek, but the eyes. Because a smile is not just a muscle movement, but an outward emotional sign, they are very hard to fake. If someone is smiling at you, but they have no wrinkles or creases around their eyes, then the smile is fake. This is one of the biggest indicators of someone who is uncomfortable in a current scenario: they smile with their lips, but their cheeks are not contracting enough to push the skin around their eyes upwards. If you are wondering if someone's happiness you see on their face is genuine, pay attention to the corners around and bags underneath their eyes.

Some people will attempt to overcompensate when they are lying. If someone is making too much eye contact, or has a very stiff upper body, that is an indicator of someone who is attempting not to fidget. For some people, they understand that unnecessary fidgeting is a powerful indicator of lying, so they will take drastic steps in order to reduce the fidgeting. But, that stiffness and the intentional eye contact that will make *anyone* uncomfortable is just as indicative of a lying state as someone who can't stop fidgeting with the hem of their blouse.

But, these nonverbal cues have to be paired with the context of the situation in order to be interpreted accurately. If you are conversing with someone, keep in mind that liars have a tendency to know and offer more details of their story. Because it's fabricated in some way, they will either answer your questions with other questions in order to give them time to come up with something, or they have already concocted a story in order to answer all your questions.

The brain is naturally an object that discards things that it doesn't deem important, which is why witness testimony is not always 100% accurate in a court. Someone telling a story of someone they met on the street might say the person's eyes were brown, and then retell it and say they were hazel. They aren't lying, it's just not important.

However, if someone is telling the same story and they talk about how the person's eyes were brown, but they were mesmerizing because they had some yellow specks in them and they thought it was odd because the little girl whose hand he was holding had blue eyes... that should cause an eyebrow to raise.

When you are analyzing someone, body language is just a percentage of what you are really taking in. Being able to analyze someone accurately takes the ability to deduce not only the person and their actions, but also their colloquialisms, as well as their emotional state, in the contextual atmosphere you find yourselves in. For example, someone who is in a bar and sweating at their brow while answering your questions might just be metabolizing their alcohol, but if that sweating is coupled with a lack of eye contact, stumbling over their words, and shortness of breath, you might be inclined to think they are uncomfortable or lying.

Some might say, "well, he's just drunk," but if you don't detect his body movements as languid and if he isn't slurring his words, then there's a good chance he has not had enough alcohol to impede his body in the way his nerves are.

All of that has to be taken in at once before you can accurately discern what is happening to the person in front of you.

When analyzing someone, you have to look at their behaviors, their eye contact, the answers they give to your questions, the timing and consistency of those answers, and their vocal characteristics, when they talk with you. All of this culminates into a deduction that will be as accurate as possible, without actually having any confirmation from the person themselves.

One thing a person has to overcome before they can even begin this journey, is their own psychological biases. These can wreak havoc on your ability to accurately deduce anything about a situation. Think of psychological biases as the complete opposition of common sense and clarity: if you have a bias, you obviously can't make an accurate assessment

… which is what you need if you are going to deduce anything about anyone at any point in time.

There are five basic psychological biases you will have to work to overcome before you can begin the journey of reading people. The first is the most common. Confirmation biases happen when you only see what you want to see, to support an existing belief you already have. For example, if you go into an interrogation room thinking someone is guilty, you will weigh their answers and their actions against the idea that you are looking for proof instead of answers.

Confirmation bias has a drastic effect in how you interpret the environment around you.

In order to avoid confirmation biases, either find other sources of information around you, take a look at the situation from multiple perspectives, or find someone to talk to about your analysis.

Anchoring is also a common form of bias. This is simply when someone jumps to conclusions. You end up making a final decision too early in the game, and it hinders your ability to make accurate decisions. Try to keep yourself from piecing together the puzzle you think you see too quickly. If you feel under pressure to make a quick decision, find a way to lengthen the time you have to make it.

If someone is pushing you too hard for a decision, then you can interpret that scenario all on its own… and usually, that person pushing too hard is pushing for their own ulterior motives.

Next, we have the overconfidence bias. This comes into play whenever someone has gotten good at what they do and has essentially gotten pompous. When someone puts too much faith in themselves and their knowledge of others, they believe they can accurately draw conclusions with very little data. This also results in the person believing their contribution to the decision is much more valuable than it really is.

This one is usually paired with anchoring, where someone who is overconfident in their abilities acts on hunches they have, rather than information they have already discovered, in an attempt to solve something before someone else does. This is a dangerous combination, and one way you can eliminate it is to ask yourself some questions: Who else is gathering information besides you? Have you talked to them about your information? Have you asked them what they found? What sources have helped you find your information? Are they reliable sources? Asking yourself some of these questions will help to keep your head in the game if you sense you are becoming overconfident.

Then, there's the gambler's fallacy. This means someone is expecting past events to influence the future. For example, if you are tossing a coin in the air and you have gotten heads 12 times in a row, that person will begin to believe they have a higher chance of getting heads than tails, when that is not the case. With a coin toss, the odds are always 50/50, and the outcome once the coin has been tossed has no influence on those odds at all.

This is the psychological bias that is the most dangerous, because people are much more willing to take greater risks if they have had success in the past. This means that, if the person fails for any reason, their fall back down to the ground is a hard and cold one. A great example is investing in a volatile and high-stakes market economy. If you had two previous investments that did well, you will assume you know how to control your outcome, when really, you don't. Then, when you make this larger account based on your prior pattern of success, you are less willing to look at the original odds of success, and more willing to look at your own successes to gauge your decision-making.

To avoid this, do not look at information in a chronological order. Instead, look at specific trends from purely a numbers angle. The more logical you can be, the better you can become at avoiding this very dangerous psychological phenomenon.

The last one is the fundamental attribution error, and this is when someone blames others when things end up going wrong. When someone fails and doesn't want to look at the situation objectively, it means they are more willing to blame someone else... or some mysterious outside force... for their failure.

A good illustration of this is a car accident: if someone rear-ends someone else, the person who got rear-ended is probably very quick to jump to the conclusion that the person who hit them is a bad driver. To them, it doesn't matter that the light was green but they weren't moving, all that matters was that they were hit, and it's that person's fault they were hit.

When we blame someone else for our mistakes, we can't learn. If you blame someone else for a wrong deduction you make about someone, then you can't look back to figure out what you analyzed wrong.

Avoiding this bias is very fluid because it means simply looking at a situation non-judgmentally. This is a bias that is warded off by developing emotional intelligence, or the ability to utilize empathy in order to understand why someone is behaving the way they are. Emotional intelligence will keep you in check with your own behaviors and actions, and empathy will allow you to emotionally tap into other people's behaviors and actions.

But, even with all this information, sometimes you just don't have the ability to spend an hour conversing with someone in order to make your deductions. Making snap decisions based on isolated data, in a span of under 5 minutes, is called "cold reading," and it takes a great deal of practice to be able to develop this art.

Chapter 4: What Is Cold Reading?

If you've ever been to a fortune teller, or seen one of those television programs that has someone standing in the middle of the floor and rattling off facts about someone that is seemingly a stranger, then you have experienced what it means to witness (or be a part of) a cold reading.

It is a wonderful phenomenon developed by people who have been analyzing individuals and their reactions to specific questions and statements for years. It is a finely-tuned skill that takes a great deal of unbiased analyzation and focus.

The person doing a cold reading doesn't just look at a person's body language or facial expression, they also look at their age, their clothing choices, their hairstyle, their gender, and even their ethnicity, in order to hone in on seemingly private and obscure facts.

They ask broad questions that allow them to tailor down their answers, and they watch how someone responds with their answers, in order to make educated analyzations. These observations help the cold reader to take the conversation in a direction that is suitable to them.

For those seeking to do cold reading for entertainment, it's possible to woo a crowd with its magic-like qualities. But, when it comes to analyzing a person and learning more about them, cold reading allows someone to be able to steer a conversation away from uncomfortable topics, and even allows someone to be able to garner more information than someone is willing to give upfront.

Cold reading is becoming a widely used phenomenon in interrogation rooms across the globe, and some lawyers are beginning to learn the technique for their courtroom interrogations. One of the most popular cold reading techniques is something called the Forer effect. It simply refers to the act of making a very vague and general statement that can apply to many people, but feels as if someone has sensed something personal about you.

For example, if you are sitting across the table from someone who doesn't make very good eye contact when they are talking, always seems to ramble themselves off-track in regard to the main subject, and sometimes fiddles with their fingers, then you might use that as a means to get to this: "It seems to me like you're sometimes insecure, especially with people you don't know very well. Am I making you uncomfortable? Because I don't mean to."

Not only has their body language portrayed to you that they might be uncomfortable, you have made a generalized statement "about them" that actually includes just under half of the world's population.

Even if the body language they are exhibiting is not because they feel uncomfortable with you, you have a high-probability of pegging them as someone with social anxieties. This makes the person more willing to trust you, because in their eyes, they see you as someone who "sees beneath the act."

Another example: If you are engaging in conversation with someone who seems sad, then you might take note of their body language. Their eyes might be glossed over, or possibly teary, and their shoulders might be slumped. Maybe their voice is lower than usual when they speak, and for the most part they aren't responsive.

Then, their phone rings and you see them grimace at the screen before silencing the ringer. In this instance, cold reading can be used to get them to open up and talk with you.

Taking all of that into account, you might be prompted to say something like this: "You're having problems with a friend or family member, aren't you?"

In fact, you actually have no idea if that's what's going on. But, out of all the possibilities, coupled with them silencing their phone, there's a very good chance that the person they are upset with was the one calling. Also, out of all the people every person knows, over 80% of them fall under either the "family" or "friend" category.

Cold reading is the interpreting of a situation with the intention of leading the conversation, in order to get information from someone who is unwilling to talk. Yes, it can be used in a crowded forum for the shock-and-awe aspect, but it's better purpose is to be used when encountering someone you want information from.

It works the same way in interrogation rooms, while being questioned on a jury stand, or even in private investigative work. Cold reading utilizes body language as well as fashion, personal grooming, and lifestyle choices in order to make deductions that pull information from someone they wouldn't always offer up on their own.

In order to begin practicing cold reading, simply sit down and have a conversation with someone. Three main topics to discuss with a new person are politics, the weather, and someone's career. After you engage with them and draw basic conclusions about their life and communication style, try using some vague statements in order to guide the conversation.

Make it a goal to see if you can get someone new to tell you about a traumatic life event that happened when they were a child. Gauge their reactions to your questions and use that as a guide, in order to sift through the barriers that they naturally put up. Just remember this: verbal cues can be just as strong as body language, so when someone is answering you, make sure you're paying attention!

Chapter 5: Verbal Cues And What They Really Communicate

Verbal communication is just as important as nonverbal communication. People who are excited don't tell a story with the same inflections and attitude as someone who is sad. Someone who is depressed doesn't use the same verbiage as someone who is happy. Sometimes even simple phrases can give away who someone has been around, and the type of influence that person has had.

Let's assume that you have the nonverbal communication analyzation techniques mastered. Hopefully you have gotten pretty good at these techniques. You now understand how to tailor your communication style to someone, or even lead the conversation, in order to get them to open up about something private. Now comes the time where you begin analyzing how someone responds to you.

Because verbal answers are just as important as nonverbal cues.

The first thing to consider is how they sound when they are answering. If their answers are short, clipped, murmured, or even yelled, you can draw a basic assumption that they are upset. You don't understand what range of "upset" they are, but you know the mood is negative. That's a start. On the other side, if someone's voice is light, airy, or has a "chipper" tone to it, you can draw the basic assumption that the mood is positive.

Now it's time to take a look at the words and phrases they are using. People who are in generally happy moods, or have no reason to lie, have smoother speech patterns. They will naturally truncate words, such as "can't" and "haven't", and they are more prone to staying on topic. Even if the topic veers off path, someone who is telling the truth (or in an overall good mood) can easily steer the topic back to where it was.

However, if someone is lying, they might be more prone to using the full word instead of its truncation. Using an overabundance of "cannot" and "have not" can signal to you that someone is being deceitful because that person is actively attempting to put up a nice facade. This overcorrection in their speech patterns is a red flag to those assessing communicative speech patterns for signs of lying and deceit.

Swift changes of a topic that never veer back to the original question is another sign of deceit, but it can also be a sign of someone becoming uncomfortable with the current topic of conversation. This is when the situational context comes into play: if you're interrogating someone and you ask a question, their avoidance of the question can be interpreted as deceit. However, if you are simply talking with someone and ask a sensitive question, their sidestepping could be interpreted not as guilt or deceit, but as a subject they would rather not discuss.

Another sign of someone telling the truth is the fact that they can answer questions coolly. Someone who is lying will try to stall for time while they come up with their next untruth, so they might answer your question with another one of their own, or they might simply repeat the question back to you. Either way, if this happens, someone is often trying to take time to formulate an answer that is something other than the truth.

Other signs of someone being deceitful or uncomfortable with a verbal exchange are things such as stuttering and using too many filler words (such as "uh" and "um").

Figuring out whether someone is uncomfortable or being deceitful will center around your ability to assess the situation you are in and the questions you are asking. There is a difference in someone sitting on a couch with you and sidestepping the question, "How are you doing since the breakup?" and someone sitting across the table from you and sidestepping the question, "Did you take my son's toy?" One situation is a bit more personal in nature, while the other has a more formal and accusatory context.

To begin your journey with analyzing verbal context clues, begin with simply analyzing their vocal patterns. Are they yelling? Or murmuring? Maybe their voice sounds monotone, or has a bit of a hiccup when they try to talk? These are all signs of negative emotional states, and this information can guide you in what you choose to ask the person. If none of these negative emotional verbal triggers exist, then look at other facets of their words: does their speech flow freely? Is their voice projecting confidently? If so, these are all positive aspects, and can help you guide the conversation in the direction you want it to go.

Once you can accurately pinpoint emotional states based on how someone's voice sounds, you can progress to analyzing the conversational tactics they are using. Are they sidestepping questions or veering too quickly off topic? If you notice that they are, there is an underlying negative connotation happening. Start to use your situational context to try and figure out why. On the other hand, if they are fully answering questions and veering off on topics that all link back together to one another, then that means there is an underlying positive connotation!

We've talked a little bit about body language and how it plays into nonverbal cues, but we really haven't broken it down into specific things you need to keep your eyes on. Out of all the types of communication we engage in on a daily basis, body language is the one that tells the greatest truths. Fake smiles and crossed arms are just the beginning when it comes to correctly analyzing body language. Body language is so important, that entire careers have centered around people who specialize in interpreting this aspect of communication.

In other words: body language is incredibly important to understand, in order to fully analyze and interpret someone correctly from the beginning.

Chapter 6: Body Language And Analyzing Others

Before we get into the rules of body language, understand this: body language is not an exact science. These "rules" are meant to guide you with assessing everything you can take in about a person, their reactions, and your surroundings, but should in no way provide a solid foundational basis for specific theories and trains of thought.

In other words, just because someone has their arms folded does not mean they are guilty of kicking your dog.

One of the first things people assess about others are their eyes. They are the emotional connectors between two individuals, and simply the lack of eye contact (or too much eye contact) can tell a great deal about a person and their emotional states. However, there is also a basic biological rule that states that eyes tend to look in the direction of the part of the brain they are using. This is important because the part of the brain that recalls and the part of the brain that creates are situated on different sides.

So, here is where the rules of the eyes come into play: if someone is looking to their right, it means they are probably lying or storytelling. However, looking to the right can also mean someone is speculating, or talking in theories. You have to be able to gauge the situation and the conversation at hand before you jump to your own biased conclusions.

The other rule is that, if the person is looking to the left, it means they are recalling facts and being truthful. But, understand this: if someone is telling something inaccurate, but they *believe* it to be the truth, they will also look to the left to recall this information. If someone mistakes someone else's eyes for blue when they are really hazel, they will walk around absolutely believing those person's eyes were blue until they see them again.

It doesn't mean they are intentionally misleading you, it simply meant they wholeheartedly believed the false information they had was truth.

Again, this will all depend on how you gauge the conversation and the person's overall body language as well.

Other cues that the eyes can give are widening of the eyes, and pupil dilation. If someone's eyes widen, it means they are taking interest in something. They might be shocked, or even attracted, but it means their interest has truly been captured. Pupil dilation is another big eye indicator, and it can reveal a great deal about how a person is feeling towards something or someone. Pupil dilation is not something we can control, and if you are in the presence of someone and you see their pupils dilate while you are conversing with them, you can make the assumption that they are attracted to you in some way.

Just make sure there aren't also dimming lights in the environment. Don't make the assumption that every pupil that enlarges in your presence means that the individual wants to jump your bones.

There are basic rules for the mouth as well. We already have a clear understanding of the difference between a fake smile and a genuine smile, but there are other things the mouth does mindlessly, in order to showcase particular emotional states.

For example, forced laughter can mean nervousness or forced cooperation with an individual, and can indicate discomfort with a particular scenario. People can also develop nervous ticks with their lips, like biting them or licking them excessively with their tongue, if they get into a situation that makes them uncomfortable.

These can all be cues exhibited, unbeknownst to the individual, that should alert you to their uncomfortable disposition.

There are also types of smiles that can indicate specific things, such as a tight-lipped smile. This can indicate the fact that someone doesn't want to be approached, or has been approached by someone they wish to not converse with. It can also signal a sign of distrust, so if you are in a bar and approach someone who gives you a tight-lipped smile, your chances for rejection have already doubled.

The head also has particular rules when it comes to reading its movement and what that can say about someone's disposition. If someone is nodding their head in a rhythmic, slow fashion, it means they are probably paying attention to what you are saying and welcoming the information you have to give them.

However, you have to check the eyes and make sure they are engaged on you, because if the eyes are not focused on you, yet the head is still moving, this means the individual is simply trying to keep you entertained courteously while their sights are focused elsewhere.

However, if someone's head nodding becomes a bit more vigorous, it means the listener feels you have already made your point and is wanting you to hurry and wrap up your conversation. This rapid head nodding is usually indicative of someone who is losing their patience.

Head placement also comes with its own set of rules: if someone's head is held high, it means they feel confident. Whether that confidence is interpreted as good or bad (such as someone being arrogant) will be combined with how they talk and interact with others.

If their head is tilted off to the side, it usually means someone is interested and comfortable with you. Tilting the head exposes the most vulnerable part of the neck. Some scientists believe this innate showing of the neck was an ancient sign of showing trust, because it meant the person whom they were exposing their main artery to, wouldn't attempt to strike it.

However, if the head is tilted downwards, like those adults on television shows who are scolding their children above the rims of their glasses, that is usually indicative of someone who is about to give disapproval or criticism of some sort. It could also be a sign that someone does not agree with you on something, especially if a controversial subject is being talked about.

These are nowhere near all the rules of body language, but they will be enough to get you started. Commit these to memory and try using them the next time you are simply engaged in conversation. Try an experiment: not only allow yourself to be aware of the person you are speaking with, but be aware of yourself. If you tilt your head off to the side, consider your emotional disposition with the person in front of you and see if it matches up. It will be a fun experiment in not only reading others, but seeing how other people would read and interpret your actions as well.

Chapter 7: Practice Makes Perfect

Body language has its roots in differentiating between cultures. From the great story in the Bible of the Tower of Babel, all the way to modern-day interpretations of body language that vary from country to country, body language has often been how others read an individual's true intentions.

The types of bodily cues found in the Western world do not mean the same things as they do in the Eastern cultures. When people were beginning to migrate and travel, many thousands of years ago, they relied on their interpretation of body language and nonverbal cues to determine whether an indigenous people were hostile to another's presence. Because they could not communicate verbally with all the different languages in play, many individuals became very adept at interpreting body language, in order to keep their tribe safe during travels.

Now, reading body language and nonverbal cues serves many different purposes. Police officers interpret them when interrogating subjects, lawyers pay attention to it when cross-analyzing witnesses on the stand, mothers use it whenever they are raising their children, and even friends use it to interpret the emotional impact of an event on someone they care about.

Analyzing people is equal parts body language, speech, nonverbal cues, and environmental. All of these things play together to give someone the greatest possible chance of interpreting someone, how they are feeling, and what they are thinking.

Getting better at analyzing and reading people is a matter of practice. As you continue to watch people and draw your own conclusions, the scenarios you find yourself in will either reinforce or disprove the theories you concoct in your head. Part of getting better at this skill is simply doing it. Also, part of getting better at this skill is memorizing what you are looking for, so you know what type of label to put to it.

This book outlines the latter, and it is your responsibility to enact the former.

One of the most important things you can do for your journey is to get over your own personal biases. Whether you are aware of them, or whether they are unconscious, predetermined emotional and personal biases will skew your results and your observations every single time. However, there are a few things you can start doing to help get over those biases, whether you believe you have them or not.

If, for some reason, you feel you are free of personal bias completely, just indulge me for a moment and implement a few of these tactics anyway.

The first thing you can do is intentionally introduce yourself to things that go against those modern-day stereotypes. Do you believe all Californians are surfer dudes with blonde hair and no brains? Then find a girl from California who is attending school and hates the ocean. They exist, and they exist in droves. Strike up a conversation with them and get to know them. Don't try to analyze and don't try to label. Just...

take it all in. Use it to reconstruct your opinion of "Californians."

Do you believe people from the South have thick accents, wear cut-off t-shirts, and hate black people? Then sit down with a Native American southern Methodist pastor in one of the southern-most states and get to know her. Ask her questions about her faith and beliefs. Willingly introducing yourself to people who do not fit the "molds" you have conditioned yourself to believe, will help burst those personally ingrained biases you already have.

Another way to bust those personal biases is to volunteer in your community. For many, personal biases are formed when they stick with what they know: the same types of people with the same types of careers who speak the same type of language. Get into your community and volunteer some of your time at a shelter.

Maybe there is a YMCA program that invites disenfranchised youth over after school for programs until their parents get off work. Maybe there is an after-school center that runs off volunteer tutors. Get into those areas of your community you are not familiar with and immerse yourself in their world.

Sometimes busting your own biases simply means exposing yourself to other parts of the world around you... even if that world is simply 10 miles downtown.

Another way to burst those personal biases is to find people who are outside your social circle that you admire. Every single group of individuals has a figure they look up to. The issue is, those groups usually never intermingle, so those revered individuals never get the chance to break down walls we naturally throw up to separate ourselves. Maybe this admired individual has not done anything to personally help you and your situation, but you can still admire them for their words and their actions.

Find someone admired in the community who is wholly different than you. Maybe they have different political views or religious beliefs. Maybe they come from a different ethnic background or country, or even speak a different language. Expose yourself to them and work to find out why they are so respected within their community.

It will not only give you a way to cross those natural walls we all create, but it will give you a chance to admire someone you might have otherwise passed by.

Just like learning how to analyze people properly takes time, so does getting rid of personal biases. For many, these biases are learned as children and then reinforced by media and entertainment outlets that their family units habitually consume.

As a child, this is not something you can control. As an adult, however, it is your responsibility to take whatever action is necessary to destroy your own biases, should they be stepping in your way.

Different cultures, when intermingling with one another, rely heavily on bodily language as well as nonverbal cues in order to understand one another. Body language is first used to determine whether an individual is hostile, and then it is used to determine if the newcomer is welcome. When both of those initial assessments move in a positive direction, then analyzing someone becomes less about safety and more about learning about the environment around them.

Learning to analyze people is not simply about trying to figure out who is lying or who is telling the truth. Learning to analyze people is also about being respectful of other customs. It is a skill that will always require new inputs of knowledge as you are exposed to other people and cultures, and it will always be a skill that will never be 100% accurate.

But, learning how to more accurately analyze people will always give you the edge, no matter how you choose to implement the skill.

Conclusion

Thanks again for taking the time to download this book!

You should now have a good understanding of where to begin when it comes to learning how to analyze people, and be able to use the rules and suggestions outlined in this book to start your own journey of self-discovery. Analyzing others is not simply about breaking them down into their individual components and reading between the lines, it's also about understanding yourself and how you are perceived in the world. Analyzing people is not just about body language or how someone sounds when they are saying something, it is also about getting rid of your own personal biases and emotions in the moment, and practically looking at things from a structural perspective.

The suggestions at the end of each chapter are geared towards helping beginners not only learn the labels and rules they need to learn, but to also help them in implementing them during real-life encounters. Do not put yourself on the spot in the beginning, but consider people-watching instead. Sit on a park bench or in a chair at the mall and just look around you. Take in the sights and the people interacting with others, and see if you can read their basic body language as a third party looking in.

Once you can master that skill and practice discarding your own personal biases in order to draw distinct conclusions, you can transition into a one-on-one phase, where you are conversing with someone while attempting to analyze them.

Remember, this is a skill, and every skill takes practice.

If you enjoyed this book, please take the time to leave a review on Amazon. I appreciate your honest feedback, and it helps me to continue producing high quality books for people like yourself who are looking for them and the information they hold.

Simply CLICK HERE to leave a review, or click on the link: How to Analyze People[SEP]

Printed in Great Britain
by Amazon

44587926R00029